Bacon Speaks

培根永恆名句

商務印書館

Bacon Speaks 培根永恆名句

作　　者　：　商務印書館編輯部
責任編輯　：　傅　薇
封面設計　：　涂　慧
出　　版　：　商務印書館 (香港) 有限公司
　　　　　　　香港筲箕灣耀興道 3 號東滙廣場 8 樓
　　　　　　　http://www.commercialpress.com.hk
發　　行　：　香港聯合書刊物流有限公司
　　　　　　　香港新界大埔汀麗路 36 號中華商務印刷大廈 3 字樓
印　　刷　：　中華商務彩色印刷有限公司
　　　　　　　香港新界大埔汀麗路 36 號中華商務印刷大廈 3 字樓
版　　次　：　2016 年 7 月第 1 版第 1 次印刷

Contents 目錄

Knowledge is power.

知識就是力量。

MEDITATIONES SACRAE

Reading maketh a full man,
conference a ready man, and
writing an exact man.

閱讀使人博學，討論使人敏捷，寫作使人精準。

OF STUDIES

Histories make men wise; poets, witty; the mathematics, subtle; natural philosophy, deep; moral, grave; logic and rhetoric, able to contend.

歷史使人獲得智慧；詩歌使人機智幽默；
數學使人精密；自然哲學使人深沉；
倫理使人莊重；修辭使人雄辯。

OF STUDIES

Ask counsel of both times; of the ancient time what is best, and of the latter time what is fittest.

人應該察古觀今，從古代得知甚麼最好，
從現今得知甚麼最適宜。

OF GREAT PLACE

Do you know?

Francis Bacon was born
on 22 January 1561. It was the Age of
Discovery when European countries
sent ships to discover the New World.

法蘭西・培根出生於 1561 年 1 月 22 日，
當時正值大航海時代，
歐洲各國紛紛派出船隊探索新大陸。

Some books are to be tasted,
others to be swallowed,
and some few to be chewed
and digested.

有的書宜淺嚐，有的宜吞嚥，
只有少數宜細嚼，繼而吸收。

OF STUDIES

*Read not to contradict
and confute; nor to believe and
take for granted; nor to find talk
and discourse; but to weigh and
consider.*

閱讀不是為了引起矛盾和駁斥；也不是為了輕信
或盲從；更不是為了高談闊論；
閱讀是為了權衡和考慮。

OF STUDIES

If a man's wit be wandering, let him study the mathematics.

如果一個人思想散漫，那就讓他研習數學。

OF STUDIES

Studies serve for delight, for ornament, and for ability.

學習是為了樂在其中、增添光彩、提升能力。

OF STUDIES

The desire of power in excess, caused the angels to fall; the desire of knowledge in excess, caused man to fall.

天使墮落，因過份貪戀權力；
凡人墮落，因過份沉迷知識。

OF GOODNESS AND GOODNESS OF NATURE

Do you know?

He had many talents and
held many positions including scientist,
philosopher, cryptologist, statesman
and lawyer.

培根才華出眾，因此身兼多職，
包括科學家、哲學家、密碼專家、
國會議員、律師。

Natural abilities ... need proyning,
by study; and studies themselves,
do give forth directions too much
at large, except they be bounded in
by experience.

天賦需要學習來修剪；而學習本身指出的方向
太籠統，需要經驗來規範。

OF STUDIES

It is not granted to man to love and to be wise.

人不是一生下來就擁有愛人的能力和智慧。

THE ADVANCEMENT OF LEARNING

I, that desire to live to study, may not be driven to study to live.

我為了學習而生存，並非為生存而學習。

LETTER TO KING JAMES I

Discretion of speech, is more than eloquence.

慎言比雄辯更勝一籌。

OF DISCOURSE

*To speak agreeably to him,
with whom we deal, is more
than to speak in good words,
or in good order.*

和人交往時，對話酣暢比使用精妙的詞藻和
語序更重要。

OF DISCOURSE

He that hath a satirical vein,
as he maketh others afraid
of his wit, so he had need be
afraid of others' memory.

喜歡諷刺的人使人畏懼其才智，
因此也害怕別人記性太好。

OF DISCOURSE

Speech of a man's self ought to be seldom, and well chosen.

少談論自己，即使談及也要謹慎。

OF DISCOURSE

Prosperity is not without many fears and distastes; adversity not without many comforts and hopes.

繁華盛世中不乏恐懼和災難；
逆境當前也會有慰藉和希望。

OF ADVERSITY

Prosperity is the blessing of the Old Testament; adversity is the blessing of the New.

繁華是《舊約》帶來的祝福；
逆境是《新約》帶來的佳音。

OF ADVERSITY

Hope is a good breakfast,
but it is a bad supper.

希望是美味的早餐，卻不是美味的晚餐。

APOTHEGMS

The pencil of the Holy Ghost hath laboured more in describing the afflictions of Job than the felicities of Solomon.

聖靈之筆比較著意描述的，不是所羅門的福氣，
而是約伯所受的苦難。

OF ADVERSITY

Do you know?

Bacon's father was the Lord Keeper of
Queen Elizabeth I. Later in 1617,
Bacon held the same position
his father had held.

培根的父親是伊莉沙伯女王的掌璽大臣。
1617 年，培根和父親一樣獲任命掌管國璽。

... prosperity doth best discover vice, but adversity doth best discover virtue.

人的醜惡在富貴中暴露，美德卻在逆境中顯現。

OF ADVERSITY

For good thoughts (though God accept them) yet, towards men, are little better than good dreams, except they be put in act.

善意即使為上帝所接受，若沒有得以實踐，
和做夢也無甚分別。

OF GREAT PLACE

In charity there is no excess.

善舉永不嫌多。

OF GOODNESS AND GOODNESS OF NATURE

A man that hath no virtue in himself, ever envieth virtue in others.

沒有美德的人往往妒忌他人之德。

OF ENVY

Do you know?

When young Bacon met
Queen Elizabeth, she was surprised by
his smartness and called him
"the young Lord Keeper".

伊莉沙伯女王首次看到年少的培根時，
十分欣賞他的聰明機智，更稱他為
"我的小小掌璽大臣"。

Goodness I call the habit, and
goodness of nature, the inclination
… without it, man is a busy,
mischievous, wretched thing;
no better than a kind of vermin.

我會稱善行為習慣，稱善的天性為傾向⋯⋯
沒有它，人只是碌碌無為的怪物，和害蟲無別。

OF GOODNESS AND GOODNESS OF NATURE

"What is truth?" said jesting Pilate; and would not stay for an answer.

"何謂真理？" 善戲謔的皮拉特問；
卻不指望會得到答案。

OF TRUTH

*No pleasure is comparable
to the standing upon the
vantage ground of truth.*

沒有一種快樂勝過立於真理之巔。

OF TRUTH

Truth may perhaps come to the price of a pearl, that showeth best by day; but it will not rise to the price of a diamond or carbuncle, that showeth best in varied lights.

真理或可比擬名貴的珍珠，能在日間展現
最美的一面；但其價值不及鑽石和紅寶石，
因為後兩者在任何光線下都能呈現最美的一面。

OF TRUTH

Clear, and round dealing, is the honour of man's nature.

人性中最高貴的品德，就是以耿直的心行事。

OF TRUTH

But it is not the lie that passeth through the mind, but the lie that sinketh in, and settleth in it, that doth the hurt.

真正令人受傷的，不是掠過腦海的假話，
而是沉下、停留在腦中的謊言。

OF TRUTH

Mixture of falsehoods, is like alloy in coin of gold and silver, which may make the metal work the better, but it embaseth it.

各種謊言的混合就像金幣和銀幣裏的合金，
或許增強錢幣的效能，卻會貶低錢幣的價值。

OF TRUTH

*There is no vice, that doth
so cover a man with shame,
as to be found false and
perfidious.*

世上最令人感到羞恥的惡行，
莫過於被揭發虛情假意、背信棄義。

OF TRUTH

Truth emerges more readily
from error than confusion.

真理往往不是由困惑而來，
而是從錯誤中發現。

NOVUM ORGANUM

Truth is rightly named the daughter of time, not of authority.

真理孕育自時間，而非權威。

NOVUM ORGANUM

Beauty is as summer fruits,
which are easy to corrupt,
and cannot last.

美就像夏日水果，很快便腐爛，不能持久。

OF BEAUTY

That is the best part of beauty, which a picture cannot express.

美到極致，連圖畫也不足以描繪。

OF BEAUTY

Virtue is like a rich stone,
best plain set.

美德如同寶石，最適合嵌在樸素的地方。

OF BEAUTY

Do you know?

Bacon entered Cambridge University
at the age of 13 but only stayed
for 3 years, for he did not like
Cambridge's scholastic philosophy
which disregarded scientific research.

培根 13 歲入讀劍橋大學，但只住了 3 年，
因不滿當時的經院哲學輕視科學研究。

For the most part beauty makes a dissolute youth, and an age a little out of countenance.

美貌總是令人在年輕時放蕩，年老時愧悔。

OF BEAUTY

Age appeared to be best in four things: old wood best to burn, old wine to drink, old friends to trust, and old authors to read.

在以下四個方面，年老是一件好事：
老木頭最適合燃燒，老酒最香醇，
老朋友最值得信任，老作家寫的書最好看。

APOTHEGMS

Houses are built to live in, and not to look on; therefore let use be preferred before uniformity, except where both may be had.

房屋是用來住的，不是用來看的；因此，
實用比外貌勻稱更重要，除非可以兩全其美。

OF BUILDING

A wise man will make more opportunities, than he finds.

智者所創造的機會比尋到的機會更多。

OF CEREMONIES AND RESPECTS

For if he labour too much to express good forms,
he shall lose their grace.

表現儀態太刻意，便有失優雅。

OF CEREMONIES AND RESPECTS

*A man would die, though he were
neither valiant, nor miserable,
only upon a weariness to do the
same thing so oft, over and over.*

人如果不斷重複做同一件事情，
即使非威武或可悲之人，也會因疲累致死。

OF DEATH

Death... openeth the gate to good fame, and extinguisheth envy.

死亡是通往名氣的大門，
也是杜絕妒忌的閘門。

OF DEATH

It is as natural to die as to be born; and to a little infant, perhaps, the one is as painful as the other.

生和死都是自然不過的事，或許對嬰兒來說，生和死一樣痛苦。

OF DEATH

Men fear death as children fear to go in the dark; and as that natural fear in children is increased by tales, so is the other.

人怕死就像小孩怕黑一樣，
故事會令孩子更怕黑，令人更恐懼死亡。

OF DEATH

It is a miserable state of mind to have few things to desire and many things to fear.

渴望的事物甚少，
畏懼的事物卻很多 —— 這種心境是可悲的。

OF EMPIRE

Do you know?

Some people believe
Bacon to be the author of William
Shakespeare's plays.

有人認為莎士比亞的作品其實出自培根。

Fortune is like the market,
where, many times,
if you can stay a little,
the price will fall.

幸福像市集，只要你多留下一會兒，
價格就會下跌。

OF DELAYS

Riches are for spending.

錢是用來花的。

OF EXPENSE

Chiefly the mould of a man's fortune is in his own hands.

創造幸福的模子掌握在自己手中。

OF FORTUNE

The way of fortune, is like the Milken Way in the sky; which is a meeting ... of small stars; not seen asunder, but giving light together. So are there a number of little, and scarce discerned virtues, or rather faculties and customs, that make men fortunate.

幸運之路就像夜空中的銀河，
是一眾集合起來的小星星；若分開了便看不見，
聚在一起才會發光。同樣，一些很微小的美德、
才華或習慣，會令人交上好運。

OF FORTUNE

*If a man look sharply and
attentively, he shall see Fortune:
for though she be blind,
yet she is not invisible.*

只要敏銳、專注地觀察，
自然可找到幸運女神：因為她雖然盲目，
卻沒有隱身。

OF FORTUNE

Light gains make heavy purses; for light gains come thick, whereas great, come but now and then.

小利可聚大財；因為積少可以成多，
巨財卻不常來。

OF CEREMONIES AND RESPECTS

There is as much difference between the counsel, that a friend giveth, and that a man giveth himself, as there is between the counsel of a friend, and of a flatterer.

朋友的忠告和自我勸告有莫大差別，
正如朋友的忠告和阿諛奉承之輩的建議
也有莫大差別。

OF FRIENDSHIP

Whatsoever is delighted in solitude, is either a wild beast or a god.

在孤獨中找到快樂的，只有野獸或神明。

OF FRIENDSHIP

It is a true rule, that love is ever rewarded, either with the reciproque, or with an inward and secret contempt.

愛是有回報的，這是真理；回報可以是愛的回應，或是藏在心裏的蔑視。

OF LOVE

Wives are young men's mistresses,
companions for middle age,
and old men's nurses.

妻子是年輕男人的情人，中年男人的伴侶，
老年男人的保姆。

OF MARRIAGE AND SINGLE LIFE

Nature is often hidden,
sometimes overcome,
seldom extinguished.

人的天性往往是隱藏的，有時候可以征服之，
但幾乎不可能消滅之。

OF NATURE IN MEN

Nature is only to be commanded by obeying her.

不服從自然，則不能駕馭自然。

NOVUM ORGANUM

Whosoever is out of patience,
is out of possession of
his soul.

任何失去耐性的人，就是失去自己的靈魂。

OF ANGER

Do you know?

Bacon had been to Blois, Poitiers, Tours, Italy and Spain where he studied the languages, politics and diplomatic skills.

培根曾到過法國布洛瓦、普瓦捷、意大利和西班牙等地，學習當地語言、治國和外交技巧。

A sudden, bold and unexpected question doth many times surprise a man, and lay him open.

一個突如其來、意料之外的大膽問題，
往往使人措手不及，袒露真相。

OF CUNNING

Children sweeten labours,
but they make misfortunes
more bitter.

孩子令父母的辛勞變得甜蜜，
也令不幸更顯悲哀。

OF PARENTS AND CHILDREN

The joys of parents are secret; and so are their griefs and fears.

為人父母的愉悅是隱藏起來的；
其悲哀、恐懼也如是。

OF PARENTS AND CHILDREN

Do you know?

Bacon disagreed with Aristotle's
method of deduction. Instead,
he emphasised data collection without
any perceived theories to produce
a theory closer to the truth.

培根不認同亞里斯多德演繹法，
並主張不預設立場下搜集資料，
歸納出最接近真理的假設。

*Fame is like a river, that
beareth up things light and
swollen, and drowns things
weighty and solid.*

名氣就像河流，使輕盈、飽滿之物浮起，沉重、
結實之物下沉。

OF PRAISE

Praise is the reflection of virtue …
If it be from the common people,
it is commonly false and naught;
and rather followeth vain persons,
than virtuous.

讚賞之言反映出美德……如果是來自平民，
則通常是虛假、蓄意的，
而且讚賞的對象為庸碌之輩，而非有德之士。

OF PRAISE

Do you know?

Bacon is an important figure in scientific methodology. The Royal Society was set up by followers of his ideas.

培根對科學研究方法影響深遠，
英國皇家學會就是由培根思想的
追隨者成立的。

Base and crafty cowards,
are like the arrow that flieth
in the dark.

卑賤、狡猾的懦夫就像暗箭一樣。

OF REVENGE

... in taking revenge,
a man is but even with his enemy,
but in passing it over,
he is superior; for it is a prince's
part to pardon.

人如果復仇，等於和敵人打平手，
但放過敵人，他便更勝一籌；
因為只有王者才有這種寬宏大量。

OF REVENGE

Revenge is a kind of wild justice,
which the more a man's nature
runs to, the more ought law to
weed it out.

復仇是一種狂放的正義，人越是依天性而行，
法律越要杜絕之。

OF REVENGE

This is certain, that a man that studieth revenge, keeps his own wounds green, which otherwise would heal, and do well.

可以肯定的是，一個常常想着復仇的人，等同常常挖開傷口，不然那傷口早已痊癒。

OF REVENGE

For the rebellions of the belly are the worst.

因飢餓而起的暴亂是最難平定的。

OF SEDITIONS AND TROUBLES

Money is like muck, not good except it be spread.

金錢就像污泥，要變得有用除非散播出去。

OF SEDITIONS AND TROUBLES

Do you know?

I worked upon the true principles of
Baconian induction.
—Charles Darwin

我就是依照培根歸納法去做研究的。

—— 生物學家查理斯·達爾文

There is nothing makes a man suspect much, more than to know little.

孤陋寡聞的人常常會起疑心。

OF SUSPICION

He that travelleth into a country before he hath some entrance into the language, goeth to school, and not to travel.

從沒學習當地語言就到某國去，
那是去上學，不是去旅遊。

OF TRAVEL

If a man be gracious and
courteous to strangers, it shows he
is a citizen of the world,
and that his heart is no island,
cut off from other lands, but a
continent, that joins to them.

一個人如果優雅地禮待異鄉人，
即表示他是世界的公民，他的心不是一座孤島，
而是和其他島嶼連成一片的廣闊陸地。

OF GOODNESS AND GOODNESS OF NATURE

Travel, in the younger sort, is a part of education; in the elder, a part of experience.

旅遊於年輕人是增長知識，
於年長的人卻是增長經驗。

OF TRAVEL

Let a man beware,
how he keepeth company with
choleric and quarrelsome persons;
for they will engage him into their
own quarrels.

人們應小心不要和易怒、喜爭吵的人交朋友，
因為會被捲入他們的爭吵之中。

OF TRAVEL

There is a wisdom in this, beyond the rules of physic: a man's own observation, what he finds good of, and what he finds hurt of, is the best physic to preserve health.

除了醫學原則外，還有養生智慧：
觀察甚麼對自己有益、甚麼對自己有害，
便是保持健康的最佳養生法則。

OF REGIMENT OF HEALTH

All colours will agree
in the dark.

在黑暗中，所有顏色都是一樣的。

OF UNITY IN RELIGION

Since there must be borrowing and lending, and men are so hard of heart, as they will not lend freely, usury must be permitted.

借貸活動是無可避免的，人又是這麼鐵石心腸，不會無償借款，所以必須准許借貸。

OF USURY

Lies are sufficient to breed opinion, and opinion brings on substance.

謊話足以孕育出見解，見解可帶來實質的內容。

OF VAIN-GLORY

Seek first the virtues of the mind; and other things either will come, or will not be wanted.

首先要找到內在的善；其他想得到之物自然會過來，否則來者已不是你所渴望得到之物了。

THE ADVANCEMENT OF LEARNING

Do you know?

In his last years, Bacon was in debt and
forbidden to hold official positions.
He then returned home where he
concentrated on writing and studying.

培根晚年債台高築，後來被禁止擔任公職，
於是居家潛心著述。

Certainly, men that are great lovers of themselves, waste the public.

太愛自己的人必定對公眾有害。

OF WISDOM FOR A MAN'S SELF

Be so true to thyself,
as thou be not false to others.

做人既要忠於自己，又不對別人虛情假意。

OF WISDOM FOR A MAN'S SELF

Men must know, that in this theatre of man's life it is reserved only for God and angels to be lookers on.

人必須明白，人生的舞台只是留給
上帝和天使觀賞的。

THE ADVANCEMENT OF LEARNING

*He that cannot contract
the sight of his mind as well
as disperse and dilate it,
wanteth a great faculty.*

一個懂得傳播並擴張自己的思想、
不會收窄思維視野的人，
對能力抱有極大的野心。

THE ADVANCEMENT OF LEARNING

If a man will begin with certainties, he shall end in doubts, but if he will content to begin with doubts, he shall end in certainties.

如果一個人開始時有十足把握，終結時必定充滿
疑惑；但如果他不介意從疑惑開始，
那麼終結時就會把握十足。

THE ADVANCEMENT OF LEARNING

Many a man's strength is in opposition, and when that faileth, he grows out of use.

很多人只在對抗時充滿力量，
失去對手後，他也成了無用之人。

OF FACTION

Do you know?

In April 1626, Bacon died of pneumonia due to an experiment of using snow for preserving meat.

培根進行冷凍防腐實驗時受寒，於一六二六年四月因肺炎去世。

Judges must beware of hard constructions and strained inferences; for there is no worse torture than that of laws.

法官必須注意無理的言辭和牽強附會的推斷；
因為沒有比扭曲法律更差的曲解了。

OF JUDICATURE

Judges ought to be more learned than witty, more reverent than plausible, and more advised than confident. Above all things, integrity is their portion and proper virtue.

法官狡猾多謀不如廣博多聞，
花言巧語不如恭敬虔誠，
過份自信不如深思熟慮。最重要的是，
要以誠信為本。

OF JUDICATURE

Ambition is like choler; which is an humour that maketh men active, earnest, full of alacrity, and stirring, if it be not stopped.

野心就像膽汁；即一種使人活躍、認真、
敏捷的體液，若不節制，則使人暴躁。

OF AMBITION

Man seeketh in society comfort, use and protection.

人於社會是為了尋找安穩，
發揮才能，得到保護。

THE ADVANCEMENT OF LEARNING

It is a strange desire, to seek power, and to lose liberty; or to seek power over others, and to lose power over a man's self.

想得到權力，卻失去自由；
或者，想得到控制別人的權力，
卻失去控制自我的權力，這種慾望真是奇怪。

OF GREAT PLACE

Nobility of birth commonly abateth industry.

世襲的貴族身份往往使人怠惰。

OF NOBILITY

Do you know?

The modern artist Francis Bacon, who was famous for his distinctive style in paintings, was named after his great ancestor Francis Bacon.

　現代著名藝術家法蘭西・培根是培根同名同姓的後代，以畫作風格強烈著稱。

They are ill discoverers that think there is no land, when they can see nothing but sea.

看見大海一望無際就以為沒有陸地的人，
都是不稱職的發現家。

THE ADVANCEMENT OF LEARNING

It is impossible to advance properly in the course when the goal is not properly fixed.

一開始訂下錯的目標，便不可能走上對的道路。

NOVUM ORGANUM

It is as hard and severe a
thing to be a true politique,
as to be truly moral.

要成為一個真正的政治家，
和成為一個真正的有德之士，
是同樣困難且嚴峻的。

THE ADVANCEMENT OF LEARNING

He that will not apply
new remedies,
must expect new evils.

不用新藥的人必然會患上新病。

OF INNOVATIONS

Do you know?

In his conversations he contemned
no man's observations, but would
light his torch at every man's candle.
—William Rawley

培根聊天時從不會詆毀他人的看法，
卻會用自己的火把燃亮別人的蠟燭。

—— 傳記作家威廉・羅利

The real and legitimate goal of the sciences is the endowment of human life with new inventions and riches.

科學真正而且合理的目的，
是為人類生命賦予新發明和財富。

NOVUM ORGANUM

Young men are fitter to invent,
than to judge; fitter for execution,
than for counsel; and fitter for new
projects, than for settled business.

年輕人宜創造，不宜批評；
宜執行，不宜提供計謀；宜開發新項目，
不宜做已有既定規限的事。

OF YOUTH AND AGE

A man must make his opportunity, as oft as find it.

每逢機會來臨，必須好好把握。

THE ADVANCEMENT OF LEARNING

Do you know?

A Dictionary of the English language
might be compiled from
Bacon's works alone.
—Samuel Johnson

要編出一部英文字典，
只需要集合培根的作品。

——字典編纂家塞繆爾・約翰遜

Bacon's Works

培根名著

陳列類別：英語學習　　HK$ 48.00

ISBN 978 962 07 4545 4

9 789620 745454

商務印書館（香港）有限公司

http://www.commercialpress.com.hk